LADYGRIM

"Don't Hate What You Create."

by Demitri

DORRANCE
PUBLISHING CO
EST. 1920
PITTSBURGH, PENNSYLVANIA 15238

Dorrance Publishing Co
585 Alpha Drive
Pittsburgh, PA 15238
Visit our website at *www.dorrancebookstore.com*

ISBN: 979-8-8872-9156-7
eISBN: 979-8-8872-9656-2

LADYGRIM

"Don't Hate What You Create."

THE LADY WENT INSIDE OF HER DAUGHTER'S ROOM WHILE SHE was in school. She destroyed the doorknob lock with a hammer. The lady walks around the room and drags everything to the ground but then stumbles upon a diary that belonged to her daughter. The lady sits down on her daughter's bed and reads her diary suddenly getting flustered by a line she read saying, "Mother is a spider with bright green eyes, but no longer am I trapped in her web of lies!" The lady starts to furiously rip out pages from the diary and stops when she sees a page with words written in large bold letters saying "GOODBYE MOTHER!" The lady paused in confusion, staring at the page until she hears a creak behind her. The lady looks behind her to see her daughter creeping silently, but before the lady can even panic and react, the daughter pulled both of the lady's eyes right out of her sockets.

The lady screams in agony and calls out, "SlllLLLL!¡"

The daughter laughs as she stuffs the lady's eyeballs in her mouth and pulls the lady's hair up with one hand, holding a butcher knife with the other.

"I hope now you can see your lies clearly in there, Mother!" the daughter says as she grips her mother's hair tighter and slices the middle of her neck, taking her mother's head completely off.

The daughter smirks, feeling her mother's blood squirt on her face as she watches her body fall to ground. "Bleed like me."

"Whoa...what a nightmare," the little girl, Sia says as she wakes up from a deep sleep. "GRANDMA!" She calls out from the bedroom.

Her grandmother goes into the little girls room, yawning and holding a cup of coffee.

"What is it Sia?" the grandmother, Eva, says as she sits next to the Sia.

"I had a really bad dream, the girl was mad at her mother and she did... really bad things to her," Sia said to Eva nervously.

"It was just a bad dream, Sia. I had one too of your grandpa giving me a Charlie horse while trying to massage my back, very painful!" Eva says laughing while slowly getting Sia out of bed "I made breakfast, come to the kitchen and I'll make you a plate."

As high spirited as she could be, Sia gets out of bed, gets situated, dressed, then walks out of her room, goes to the dining table, and sits next to her grandpa, John.

"Good morning pumpkin," says John to Sia, rubbing her back gently.

Sia was lost in thought as if she was in her fourth daydream, disregarding John's "good morning" and Eva dropping her plate of breakfast right in front of her.

"Eva, can you get me some more milk from the store for my coffee, dear?" John said to Eva.

"Sure honey, I'll be right back," Eva says to John as she grabs her keys and steps outside to the store.

The grandpa gives Sia a look of concern and slowly grips her hand.

"How is it up there in space? I'm seventy-four years old but I've never been where you are now," John says, chuckling, forcing a smirk on Sia's face.

"Grandpa... what does it mean when someone says 'Bleed like me'?" Sia asked, nervously awaiting John's response.

"Hmm, where did you hear that from?" John asked as he pondered on Sia's question.

"I had a horrible dream last night and the girl said it to her mom after she..." Sia said, trying her best not to go into too much terrifying details.

"I see, it sounds to me like the daughter is jealous of her mother's blood because she's eating healthy or something so the mother got sick of her daughters nonsense, but it's only a dream so I wouldn't think about it too much," John said, trying to bring some humor into the conversation.

"Is that what Mom did to me too?" Sia asked John anxiously.

John looks at Sia with a mouth full of words he knew he couldn't release. Just then, Grandma Eva walks in the house with groceries.

"I'm back!" Eva announced as she stares at both plates of breakfast noticing that Sia has a full plate. "Sia! You haven't even touched your food, how are you supposed to focus in school when you have both the teacher and your stomach talking to you at the same time?" Eva exclaims, folding her arms.

"I guess I wasn't hungry. I'm late for school anyway, so I'll see you later," Sia says as she gets up from the dining table, puts on her bookbag, and rushes out the front door.

Eva pours herself and John another cup of coffee and sits next to him.

"What's gotten into that little girl? This was perfectly good breakfast," Eva says to John as she digs into Sia's plate of breakfast.

"She's growing up, eventually she has to know the truth, Eva," John says to Eva, giving her a serious stare.

"Hmph," Eva huffs and puffs rolling her eyes at John.

Sia is a fifteen-year-old girl who is usually timid and keeps to herself most of the time due to the fact that she feels like nobody understands her. She lives with her grandparents and has lost a lot of her memory of when she was younger due to what was known as a freak accident. Sia often asks about her parents and her grandparents tell her that her mother and father left her and went far away, but they will be back to rescue her. In return, Sia's grandparents will take care of her until her parents return from their mission. And to top off the stress, Sia just started high school and her main issue was becoming sociable with the other kids. Ever since she has been having these bad dreams, it's been worse socializing since being open about it makes people automatically assume that she is crazy.

The bell rings and it's lunch time, so many kids, a whole lot of noise. Timidly waiting in line, Sia grabs her lunch and sits down on a table by herself. However, though she never expected to have company, a girl sits down at Sia's table, across from her.

"Hiya!" the girl says to Sia.

"...Hey," Sia replies, staring down at her tray moving her food around.

"Let me guess, you don't like this lunch food right?" he girl says giggling as she pokes at her own food.

"No... just a lot on my mind is all. You couldn't be interested," Sia says as she continues to move her food around the tray.

"Well, NOW you got me interested and it sure beats keeping it to yourself till it drives you crazy, what's up?" the girl says, moving her tray out of the way staring at Sia in suspense.

Sia stares back at the girl, cringing. "Everyone is always interested until I finally open myself up, then it all falls down like a house of cards," Sia says, sighing.

"That's just it, I'm not everyone, so how would you know unless you try?" the girl says with a huge manipulative smile.

After verbally twisting Sia's arm, Sia sighs deeply and tells the girl in full detail about the dream she had, the girl's expression completely changed.

"Whoa... that is a very horrible nightmare. No wonder your face is as pale as the moon," the girl says, trying to maintain composure.

"It's been eating me because I get these dreams so often now and I feel like nobody tries to help me understand it. I don't even want to sleep sometimes," Sia says, looking down moving her full tray over to the side.

"Well, maybe you should lay off the scary movies. I know it's fun to sneak them from your parents, but not if you are getting those kinds of dreams," the girl says, trying to give helpful advice.

Sia smirks, looking at the girl. "If only it were that simple but I don't really watch scary movies, honestly," Sia says, chuckling.

"Not even Chuckie? He's creepy sure, but he's sorta... cute too, no?" the girl says, trying her hardest not to laugh.

Sia laughs and reaches her hand out. "You're crazy, but I like it! My name is Sia."

The girl smiles and shakes Sia's hand, "I'm Phoebe!"

Sia smiles at Phoebe.

"Nice to meet you!" Sia and Phoebe both say at the same time.

Sia and Phoebe had lunch together and exchanged cell phone numbers as they parted ways to class. Time passes and besides making her new friend, Sia had a day of school that she would call mediocre, dealing with a teacher who speaks so slow, it's like watching paint dry.

Sia tries to relieve her stress at the dinner table by talking and spending time with Grandpa John.

"So I met a new friend at school today, Grandpa," Sia says anxiously.

"Your teachers don't count as friends, Sia. They're supposed to teach you, not baby you," John says, smirking and winking at Sia.

Sia giggles. "Grandpa! She is a student who is my age and her name is Phoebe. She is also pretty nice," Sia says, smiling at John.

"Sounds like a good friend, I just hope she isn't imaginary," John says, chuckling under his breath.

Sia looks at John, smirking and folds her arms. "You know, you can be really mean sometimes Grandpa, I'm sure Mom would have liked my new friend because she's crazy like me," Sia says, jokingly sticking her tongue out at John.

John laughs. "If you mean 'go trash someone's room because I demand dominance' as crazy, then yes, her and your mom would make the best of friends," John says, chuckling some more.

Sia gives John a suspicious stare and folded her arms. "Grandpa! She is your daughter, how can you be mean to her like you are to me?" Sia says sarcastically.

John gives off a big grin, "It's all love baby, I'm going to love you but I am going to do it my own way, sarcastically. Although I joke around, I am really happy you found a good friend," John says, jokingly gripping Sia's hand softly.

"Thank you Grandpa. I guess you're not so bad for an old man after all," Sia says laughing, winking back at John.

As both Sia and John share laughter, Grandma Eva walks in with a huge tray that had three plates filled with food and started to place them.

"Dinner is ready!" Eva shouts excitedly.

Sia stuffs her face with food and was so filled, she went to her room to lay down and relax. Sia then falls fast asleep. As her sleep gets deeper, she starts to dream which... wasn't the kind of dream she would want.

A lady sits down on the dinner table with her stepson as they converse over dinner.

"Did you talk to her Paul?" the lady asked her stepson.

"I did Mom, she told me everything," Paul says to the lady nervously.

"Well spill it out! Don't keep me waiting boy or I'll tell your father what you did," The lady says, crossing her arms staring at Paul straight in the eyes.

"No please, I'll tell you! She said she got accepted to an international art school that's giving her a full scholarship and a dorm to stay in to pursue her dreams," Paul says, blank face staring at the table.

The lady smirks and bangs on the table. "And have her leave the house? I think not! I am canceling that acceptance and when she asks me what happened, I'll tell her that her brother told me all about her plans."

Paul starts to panic, "No please! She said if I told anyone, she would slice..."

In the middle of his sentence, the lady sees a knife impale Paul's eye socket through the back of his head. As Paul's blood splats on the lady's face, she stares in horror as she sees a hand pulling Paul's hair hard enough to force his mouth open Screaming in agony, Paul gets beheaded cleanly with a butcher knife leaving only the bottom of his mouth intact to the corpse. As the body falls to ground, the lady sees her daughter standing there holding a butcher knife and half of Paul's head staring at the lady dementedly.

The daughter approaches the lady and puts Paul's head close to her face and says "Traitor."

Sia wakes up drenched in sweat as well as heavy breathing in panic. "Grandpa! Grandpa!"

Suddenly, Grandpa John storms into Sia's room the same way FBI agents would kick into a house holding his trusty double barrel shotgun aiming around the room.

"First one to touch her will eat shells through both wind pipes!" John says, unaware of the situation.

Sia looks at John pale white with her hands up. "Gr..grandpa, do not shoot me, I am scared as it is." Sia says, quivering in fear.

John pauses. "You mean no one is killing you?" John says as he looks around awkwardly and slowly puts the gun down.

Sia facepalms and sighs deeply. "Grandpa, the only thing killing me are these nightmares, I can't make them stop."

John sits next to Sia, wiping the sweat off her face with his handkerchief. "Well, these nightmares are surely putting you to work out a sweat. What was it this time?"

Sia looks at Grandpa nervously, hoping he didn't ask that question. "I... don't know if you really wanna hear this in full detail Grandpa."

John chuckles, looking at his old wrist watch. "Well, it's 3:30 am and you have me and Señor Boom to your doom wide awake. I think we can handle a scary story or two."

Nervously twiddling her thumbs, Sia told John about her nightmare in full detail which wasn't the easiest thing to do. Afterwards, John gives Sia a huge look of concern as if he's heard of a dream similar to her's before.

"Wow... what is your grandma putting in your food? If that's what is causing these nightmares, I'm going on a diet," John says sarcastically, trying not to freak out from Sia's nightmare.

"Come on Grandpa, don't be so mean to Grandma. You've been eating Grandma's food longer than me, couldn't you have gotten these nightmares too?" Sia says, trying to get a straight answer from John.

John laughs, wiping the last of the sweat off Sia's face. "I guess you're right, I got nightmares too when I was about your age but it wasn't as constant and the worse one was a donkey eating every strand of hair on my head till it was so shiny, the donkey went blind when the sun reflected off of it."

Sia giggles softly, using John's nightmare to feel better about her own. "Oh Grandpa, I just don't know what to do or what it all even means."

John ponders a bit. "It's frequent so it can possibly be a message or it can mean you should frequently stop eating your grandma's cooking," John says sarcastically, chuckling under his breath.

Sia giggles again, hugging John tightly. "Thank you Grandpa. I feel better."

John tucks Sia into bed, kissing her forehead. "Well, that makes one of us because I have to release your grandma's food in the toilet. Goodnight pumpkin," John says as he slowly runs, holding his butt cheeks together.

"Goodnight Grandpa!" Sia says, giggling as she slowly falls to sleep.

Morning arrives and Sia wakes up late for school. Feeling tired from last night, Sia does her best to get dressed and prepare herself even though time wasn't on her side. Passing through the kitchen, Grandma Eva says her good mornings to Sia and offers her breakfast which Sia kindly declines and races out the door. Sia gets to school fifteen minutes late to her class only to find out that there is a substitute teacher sitting at her teacher's desk.

"Good morning. Ms. Janey is sick today so we are watching a movie until the end of class, please take your seat," says the substitute teacher as she prepares the movie for the class.

Sia takes her seat and begins to match the movie. Ten minutes into the movie, Sia starts to get drowsy due to her lack of sleep last night and lays her head on her desk, slowly nodding off. However, what she didn't expect was being drowned into yet another nightmare.

A lady spends time with a beautiful girl, Carol, with a pink semi short dress, pink and white heels, and long blonde hair, having drinks in the lady's daughter's room.

"Wow Carol, you look so beautiful in your dress!" the lady says to Carol, admiring the fabric design of her dress.

"Thank you! It was such a generous, expensive gift you've given me," Carol says, modeling herself around the room.

"It was my pleasure. I only used the money her father kept sending for her for the past twelve years. It looks better on you than it will ever look on her," the lady says, smirking as she watches Carol model around the room.

"That girl has no sense of style. I don't know how you can even hang around her," Carol says to the lady as she looks at herself in the mirror.

"I don't hang around her, she's embarrassing which is why you are my real daughter, not that piece of shit her father gave me," the lady says, staring at Carol through the mirror going through her daughter's accessory box. The lady pulls out a silver necklace filled with diamonds that was bought for the daughter by her father and puts it around Carol's neck.

"Wow! This is so beautiful! I am utterly speechless!" Carol says, excited to model the diamond necklace around her neck.

"Anything for my real daughter," the lady says, admiring Carol through the mirror.

"That sounds nice. That means I should start calling you 'Mom' from now on, right?" Carol says, winking at the lady through the mirror.

"That's a great idea, you should from now on," the lady says, winking back at Carol.

"Okay Mo..."

As Carol was getting ready to finish her sentence, a harpoon pierces through the mirror, penetrating completely through Carol's upper abdomen. As Carol's blood splatters all over the face of the lady, the daughter reveals herself behind the mirror and in front of Carol. Carol lifelessly stares at the daughter, crying in utter terror as the daughter grips Carol's long blonde hair by the roots and starts to carve the outskirts of Carol's face with a scalpel. The lady is completely terrified as she hears Carol's screams of agony. The daughter carves

Carol's face completely and rips Carol's face from her skull and stares at the mirror.

"Ahh Carol, that face lift makes you look so beautiful now," the daughter says, twisting the harpoon slowly in Carol's upper abdomen.

Carol uses the last of her strength to scream as the daughter pulls out the butcher knife, grips Carol's hair, and slices her head off, leaving Carol's neck exposed. As blood starts to sprinkle from the inside of Carol's neck, the daughter takes off the diamond necklace from Carol's corpse and puts it on, along with Carol's face that was carved on top of her own face and walks towards her mother.

"Aren't I pretty enough to be your real daughter now?" The daughter says as the lady stares at her with paralyzing fear. The daughter raises the butcher knife at the lady. "I'll show you how to accept!"

Sia wakes up in class drenched in sweat and her hair frizzy enough to look like she has gotten struck by lightning. Sia looks around the class to notice that everyone is staring and laughing at her, including the substitute teacher. Sia turns as red as a full bottle of ketchup and runs out of the classroom heading inside the nearest girls' room. She looks at herself through the mirror to witness what has become of her after her nightmare.

"Why is this happening to me?" Sia says to her reflection, nearly in tears.

Suddenly, Sia hears someone slowly walking towards the girls' bathroom and runs into one of the bathroom stalls.

"Oh boy, I hate science. Omar's breath makes my nose runny," says the girl to herself in the bathroom, running her hands under cold water.

Sia recognizes that voice but wasn't too sure, so she looked under the bathroom stall door. Through the mirror reflection, she saw that it was Phoebe fixing her hair, talking to herself. Sia unlocks the door and slowly walks out of the bathroom stall, revealing herself to Phoebe.

Phoebe looked at Sia wide-eyed. "Sia? Who died and made you Frankenstein?" Phoebe says, bursting out in laughter.

Sia's face turns all red as she looks down in embarrassment. "Come on Phoebe, it's not my fault this happened to me," Sia says, blushing in embarrassment.

"I understand, Sia. The blowdryer can be a very dangerous thing." Phoebe says, giggling and poking at what seems to be Sia's big afro.

Sia slaps Phoebe's shoulder. "Would you quit it Phoebe? This happened after I slept in class and had another one of those nightmares I have."

Phoebe gasps as she gives Sia a huge look of concern. "Are you telling me that the teacher tased you for sleeping in class?" Phoebe says in shock.

Sia facepalms and sighs deeply. "Nevermind. What are you even doing here anyway? I didn't see you use the toilet," Sia says, folding her arms.

"Uh... my classmate was making me suffocate with his breath so I came here in case I had to vomit." Phoebe says, trying to plead her case.

Sia laughs. "And how did the teacher feel when you told him that's the reason you are going to the bathroom?"

Phoebe shrugs her shoulders. "Was he supposed to know where I am? Well, what he doesn't know won't kill him, right?"

Sia shakes her head as both her and Phoebe share laughter.

After leaving the girls bathroom and splitting up with her friend, Sia decides to sneak out of school early to avoid any more laughter from her classmates.

Thinking of excuses to tell her grandparents, Sia finally makes it home where Grandma Eva hears her coming in through the front door and looks at the time on the microwave.

"Sia? You're home early today. Is everything okay?" Eva says, washing dishes in the kitchen.

Sia makes a quick pause. "Yeah Grandma, we just had a half of a day that's all" Sia says quickly and nervously.

As Sia tries to rush to her room, Grandpa John blocks her path unintentionally and looks at her.

"Whoa, is the circus in town? They're gonna love this look on you," John says, chuckling to himself.

Grandma Eva then comes out of the kitchen to see what has become of Sia.

"Good heavens, Sia. Did your head get stuck in a cotton candy machine?" Grandma Eva says, poking Sia's massive afro.

Sia's face turns as red as a stop sign and suddenly bursts in anger. "You guys are just as bad as those idiot kids at school!" Sia shouts as she storms into her room and slams the door.

Both Grandma Eva and Grandpa John felt terrible about making fun of Sia's appearance, especially not knowing her situation. After quick discussion, Eva goes to Sia's room to talk to her.

"Honey?" Eva says, lightly knocking on her door.

"Go away Grandma. I've had enough of your jokes for one lifetime," Sia says from the other side of the door.

"I was wrong and I shouldn't have done that. Can we talk please?" Eva says sincerely.

Sia sighs deeply and opens the door for Eva, then she storms back to her bed angrily. Grandma Eva looks at Sia, feeling as guilty as ever, and slowly walks into her room and sits next to her.

"Can you tell me how this happened to your hair and why your school clothes are all sweaty?" Eva says, softly rubbing Sia's back.

Sia slowly looks at Grandma with bloodshot eyes. "You wouldn't believe me if I told you."

Eva smiles at Sia, rubbing her back some more. "Try me! If you hold it in, it only makes you feel worse," Eva says with confidence.

Feeling Eva's confidence, Sia decides to tell Grandma a little about the nightmare she had and why that caused her to make up looking the way Sia did. However, Eva felt skeptical.

"You're overreacting a little too much on these 'nightmares'. Watch some TV or something to get your mind off of these things," Eva says, attempting to be helpful in her own way.

Sia felt internally crushed by Eva's skepticism but didn't show it. She just turned on the television and started flipping through channels. Grandma Eva smiles and kisses Sia's forehead.

"I'll start making some food in the kitchen if you need me." Eva says as she walks out of Sia's room.

Sia rolls her eyes. "Yeah, whatever," Sia says as she continues to flip through channels. She stopped flipping channels when the news came on as she took interest in it.

"Breaking news! The serial killer famously known as LadyGrim strikes again killing five more people, three boys and two girls, in their sleep at the same time around the Saint Pete region. Police say that these people seized to death in their sleep while professionals working on this case a long time know that the seizing is caused from head trauma due to strange and deadly nightmares. Outrageous as that sounds, a Ladygrim survivor spoke to the press after allegedly seizing and waking up before she could kill him in his sleep," says the newscaster reporting the news.

They then showed a man in his late twenties, who looked both sleep deprived and malnourished, giving a speech. "I saw her! Lurking in the shadows looking for her next victim. I always feel her terror and it causes me to sweat ridiculously every time she shows up in my dream. I was lucky enough to see her up close and live to tell the tale, but with unfortunate consequences. She had my best friend by the neck, pulled out a butcher knife, and sliced his head off, laughing as blood spewed out of his neck like a water fountain. Only half of her face looked... human but it was hard to see past her popping out my best friend's eyes out of his head and squeezing them in her hands until they burst like grapes. I remember he once told me that she was haunting his dreams for months prior to this happening to him. Makes me wonder if she is alive looking to take lives or is she dead looking to take souls... perhaps both? Either way, she is the type to scare you whether you are alive or dead," says the LadyGrim victim in his speech.

Sia pondered the speech, knowing that his dreams sounds very similar to her own. The reporter then returns to the screen.

"Rumor has it that LadyGrim puts you in a series of dreams before she locks you in a deep sleep, killing you in your nightmare while she wears all black... like the grim reaper. The biggest question always remains, if LadyGrim is haunting and killing people in their sleep, how is she doing so in the mental institution that she is currently in with no access to the outside world? I guess only time will tell us all. Until then goodnight, sleep tight, and don't let the LadyGrim bite."

Sia then flicks the television off and ponders, "LadyGrim? If I am getting the same dreams that man was getting, that means it's only a matter of time before it starts to get dangerous for me. They said she is in a mental institution so I have to find her before she finds me.

Sia rushes under her bed and takes out her laptop to start searching for mental institutions. Luckily for her, there's only one mental institution 400 miles from her current location while the rest of them are out of state or out of the country. Sia figures it has to be the one since it's the same institution shown on the news report.

As she tries to figure out how she is gonna travel there, a call from Grandma Eva is heard from downstairs, "Sia! Time to eat honey!"

Sia puts away her laptop and rushes downstairs to eat with her grandparents.

After such a huge meal, Sia feels full and excuses herself to her room. She decides to relax on her bed and watch some television after a day of mental exhaustion. Sia slowly starts to nod off watching her show. However, the show that comes with her sleep is a nightmare that seems to haunt her mental state yet again.

A lady storms upstairs to her room to speak with her husband. "She has to go, I no longer want her in my house if she is not going to listen to my commands," the lady says sternly

"Aren't you overreacting a bit? She's just trying to live her life," the husband says, taking a big gulp of his beer.

The lady folds her arms angrily. "Are you serious right now? You're gonna sit here and defend my daughter over me? I'm supposed to be YOUR wife, but something tells me you are probably screwing my daughter on the side! Piece of shit!" the lady screams while storming out of the room, slams the door, and waits by the side of her bedroom.

The husband was furious to hear what his wife said, so he guzzles the rest of his beer and storms out of the room, heading towards the daughter's room. The husband then started to take the daughter's belongings from her room, put them in bags, and tossed them out the front door. The lady chuckles, knowing this was the reaction she wanted to trigger. She then started to help her husband toss her daughter's belongings outside.

"We already have such beautiful kids. If she's not gonna take care of them, wash their clothes and ours, and make us meals day and night, we don't need this bitch taking up our space!" the lady says, comforting her angry, drunken husband.

"I don't really care! I just want her out of my house so I don't have to hear about how much you hate her anymore!" the husband shouts, throwing the last of the daughter's belongings outside.

The husband then grabs another beer and goes up to his room, slamming the door. The lady laughs hard, sitting down on her couch and watching her reality TV show. The lady suddenly hears glass shattering and really loud thumps from upstairs in her bedroom. The lady slowly goes upstairs and opens her bedroom door to see her husband sitting on the bed with a shattered beer bottle pierced through his neck, lifeless. Extremely nervous, the lady slowly steps into the room, looks around, and finds her daughter sitting by the closet door on the side of the bedroom, holding her butcher knife.

"Silver! That is enough!" the lady says to her daughter.

"Enough? This was just a warm up. The fun hasn't started yet," Silver says, smirking dementedly.

"How am I supposed to tell my four kids that their father is dead?" the lady says with anger.

Silver slowly looks at her mother and smirks, "Speaking of them, have you checked on them lately?"

The lady ponders. "Last I checked, they were eating oatmeal in the kitchen, but I haven't heard a peep from them since."

Silver laughs, "Oh mother, they didn't like your oatmeal so big sister came to the rescue and made them a fresh new yummy bowl using my... secret ingredient."

The lady's face turns pale white staring at Silver, "...you didn't."

Silver laughs some more. "Bleach has it's purposes other than just cleaning," Silver says, winking at her mother.

"I hate you!" the lady screams at the top of her lungs.

Silver stands up and slowly approaches the lady, "Don't hate what you create."

Sia wakes up sweaty enough to soak her entire bed, deeply heavily breathing. Sia then gets off her bed and runs to the restroom to immediately shower.

"Silver? That must be the actual name of this LadyGrim girl," Sia says, pondering the dream she had.

Sia finishes her shower, races to her room, and starts packing her bag with necessities while getting dressed. Once everything was complete, Sia goes downstairs and bumps into her Grandma Eva.

"Where are you off to in such a hurry? I didn't know you had school on a Saturday," said her Grandma Eva as she stares at her big bookbag full of stuff.

"No Grandma, I am going to my friend Phoebe's house to have a... slumber party," Sia says, giggling nervously.

Grandma Eva looked overjoyed. "Awww, that sounds like a lot of fun! Be sure to leave us her number in case something happens or if your phone dies and you need your grandfather to pick you up."

Sia smiles and puts Phoebe's number on her grandma's phone. "There you go Grandma. May I borrow some money in case Phoebe and her family wants to go out somewhere?"

Her Grandma Eva gives Sia a big kiss on the cheek and puts an $100 bill in her pocket. "Don't spend it all in one place sweetheart. I will call you later. Have fun!"

Sia hugs her grandma and rushes out of the front door.

After an hour of travel by foot, Sia makes it to the bus station of which takes her to the mental institution she wants to go to. Sia bought a $40 round trip ticket, entered the bus, sitting all the way in the back, and makes a phone call to Phoebe.

"Hello! This is Fee to the e to the be! Although you think I answered your call, I actually didn't, so sucks to be you! Leave a message."

Sia rolls her eyes and leaves her a voicemail. "Phoebe! It's Sia, your voicemail tricked me because I thought it was really you, idiot! I told my grandma that I was staying over your house for a slumber party so if she calls you, just stick to that story. Thanks Pheebs!"

Sia concludes her message and hangs up the phone. A boy with blue eyes and red hair about Sia's age started to converse with her.

"So you're running away too, huh?" the boy says to Sia.

Sia looks at him in confusion. "Running away? Nooo, I love my family; I am just exploring."

The boy looks intrigued by her answer. "Exploring is my favorite thing to do. Explore new places and new people."

Sia again has a look of confusion. "You like to explore new people?"

The boy smiles lightly. "Yeah, I wanna know what people like to do and what makes them bring out their pretty smile."

Sia smiles softly at the boy. "Is that so? Well, good company always makes me smile as long as I know my company's name."

The boy smiles a bit wider. "Yes, how rude of me. My name is Raul and you must be Sia."

Sia opened her eyes wide, looking at Raul. "How... did you know my name, Raul?"

Raul smirks, folding his arms. "I've been expecting you. Fate has crossed us for a severely important mission."

Sia turns pale white after hearing this and starts to shake. "Are you serious? I'm not... even ready for any important missions," Sia says, stuttering in her words.

Raul laughs and taps Sia on her shoulder. "Luckily for you, I am not serious. I know your name because I overheard you saying it while you were on the phone."

Sia turns red from embarrassment and softly punches Raul in the arm. "You Sk_a gIi_C k_e r! You scared me to death."

Raul laughs even harder while Sia awkwardly stares down, embarrassed.

"Why the hell are you even on this bus anyway?" Sia says feeling a bit annoyed.

Raul suddenly stops laughing and his face became serious. "I'm... going to... visit someone," Raul said sadly.

Sia saw that she hit a nerve and started to interrogate. "Is it your giirrrrrllllfriend?" Sia said, teasing his emotions.

Raul suddenly got defensive. "No! You... wouldn't understand."

Sia leans back and folds her arms, resting her knee while looking at Raul. "Try me. I have some psycho stories of my own."

Raul gets frustrated. "I don't need you to pretend! Leave me alone!" Raul says, moving a few seats away from Sia.

Feeling awful about what she said, Sia realized how similar Raul sounded to herself and perhaps should been more sympathetic. Sia then decides to give him his space and rest from her long journey to the bus. Exhausted, Sia decides to take a nap through the trip. What she didn't know is that her nightmares were following her.

A little girl was sitting next to her mother in her mother's bedroom. The mother was crying as she spoke with her daughter.

"Sia, it's about that time for you to be a big girl for mommy," the mother said, rubbing her daughter's back.

Sia was confused. "But Mom, I'm only four years old, I dunno how to be big girl yet," Sia says, looking at her mom.

The mother smiles at Sia with a face full of tears. "Oh yes you will learn baby girl, you're *very* smart, but Mommy has to go now, okay? Grandma and Grandpa will come pick you up in a little while," the mother says, slowly getting up.

Sia starts getting anxious. "But Mom, where are you going? Where's big sister?" Sia says, almost screaming.

Suddenly a huge thump on the ceiling can be heard as if someone broke through the roof. Both Sia and her mother jump in astonishment from the sound. The mother drags Sia into the closet and seals it shut.

"Mommy loves you sweetheart. Don't make any noise until Grandma and Grandpa show up, okay?" the mother said panicky as she stares at her bedroom door.

After hearing what sounds like large footsteps coming closer, the bedroom door was ferociously being chopped down by a butcher knife. A voice can be heard on the other side of the door.

"I know you're in there Zophie, you can't hide from me anymore," says the female voice continuously chopping the door.

"Don't do this Silver! I am your mother and I demand you stop this madness!" says Zophie in complete fear.

The door is then smashed into pieces as Silver finally enters in the bedroom holding the bloodstained butcher knife.

Zophie falls to floor and looks up at Silver. "What do you want from me? You already took everything that I have!" says Zophie, hoping to calm Silver down.

Silver looked at Zophie with a demented smile rubbing her finger through the sharp edge of the butcher knife.

"Don't play innocent with me mother, or should I even call you that?" Silver says, walking closer to Zophie.

"I gave birth to you; I gave you life. How could you do this?" Zophie says, moving back to the wall slowly.

Silver laughs hysterically. "You indeed gave me life, but at what price? Suffering? Pain? Torment? Mental abuse? You created who I am, Zophie. Aren't you proud?" Silver says as she walks slowly towards Zophie.

"There is no way I can ever be proud of a monster!" Zophie says, firmly staring into Silver's eyes.

Silver's gruesome smile suddenly changes into a serious look of death. "Well then, I guess you haven't had much time to look in the mirror, huh?" Silver says as she tightly holds her butcher knife.

Silver then lunges at Zophie and ferociously starts swinging her butcher knife all over Zophie's body.

Zophie starts screaming in agony, feeling deep cuts from the butcher knife as well as looking at the demonic look on Silver's face as she continues. Sia closes her eyes and ears in the closet after hearing Zophie's screams which eventually stopped. Sia then looks through the crack of the closet to see Silver chopping off Zophie's head from her decapitated body.

After completely beheading Zophie, Silver slices the word "Monster" on Zophie's forehead, faces her head towards a mirror, and stabs the butcher knife on the mirror through her hair so Zophie's head stays, watching itself in the mirror.

"Now you'll forever see the monster that you are," Silver says, looking at the lifeless head.

Silver then looks at the closet as if she knows someone is in there and slowly starts approaching the closet. Sia trembles in fear, trying not to make a sound. Silver stops right next to the closet.

"I feel you getting closer, I know you are lost. Once you find me, I will help find you," Silver says softly and then kicks the closet door with immense strength.

Sia suddenly wakes up feeling extremely sweaty with her hair frizzed up to the max. Sia looks around to notice Raul was staring right at her.

"Wow, that was intense. I never actually seen a chia pet grow right before my eyes," Raul says with a look of astonishment.

Sia then blushes hard and tries to cover her hair with her jacket while not making eye contact with Raul. "SHUT UP! GO AWAY! YOU WOULDN'T UNDERSTAND!" Sia says loudly, extremely embarrassed by the situation.

Raul smiles and approaches Sia while slowly taking the jacket off of her head.

"I am here to listen to you. Plus, I am definitely interested in knowing how that happened, very unusual," Raul says comfortingly and trying to be supportive.

Sia looks at Raul and tries to decipher whether or not he's being sincere or if he's setting up for something cruel, she took the benefit of the doubt to trust him.

"This all happens because of a nightmare I constantly have when I fall asleep. I have been getting these segments of a girl murdering people while a woman watched it all happen right in front of her. This one, however, felt different. This one felt like I was actually in it living through the horror," Sia says, looking down and embarrassed revealing her darkest secret to a total stranger.

Raul looks interested and continues to comfort Sia.

"That is really intense. Have you ever seen any of these people before?" Raul asks.

Sia looks up at Raul again and starts to tear up.

"No... at least I don't believe I have. My childhood is such a blur to where I don't even remember before I was ten years old. I just don't know why these nightmares are happening to me of all people," Sia says, anxiously hoping to get answers.

Raul ponders on the situation and tries to put his two cents in.

"Hmm, well I think they might be messages from another dimension. They say when you sleep or meditate, your spirit leaves the body for a period to wander and find its peaceful place. They also said that while your spirit is away from the body, another evil spirit can enter the host and manipulate them with stress, anxiety, nightmares, and all sorts of things that can cause you kill yourself," Raul says, feeling the inner geek come out of him.

Sia looks at Raul, astonished by the information he's sharing with her as she knew nothing of it.

"Wow I never knew that. Do you think maybe... an evil spirit is haunting me as I sleep?" Sia says, slowly starting to tremble.

Raul starts to ponder some more. "There's definitely a spirit messing with your sleep. The question is who is this spirit and why does this spirit wanna haunt you of all people?" Raul says, trying to figure out the missing piece of the puzzle.

Sia then remembers something that she heard on the television. "They said on TV that someone was killing people through their nightmares, they called this person LadyGrim and she is apparently alive. Is that even possible?" Sia says, trying to fill in more of the pieces.

Raul looked at Sia as if he uncovered exactly what she is going through.

"I heard about that. She has the power to go into people's minds when they are most vulnerable and weak minded. That's usually when demonic spirits, or in this case living demonic spirits, find it easiest to strike. Maybe you not remembering your memory made you an easy target," Raul says, hoping to find the answer.

Sia turns pale and starts nodding her head. "You may be right, but it feels different. She said in my dream that she feels me getting closer when I am actually going to the mental institution that she lives in. I need to confront her and end this once and for all," Sia says firmly while tying her hair up.

Raul looks shocked by her response.

"Wait a minute, you're on this bus to go see the person who is giving you nightmares so you can confront her? You gonna tell her to stop giving you nightmares or else?" Raul says sarcastically.

Sia gives a serious look to Raul. "No, I just wanna know why she's doing this to me and why did she keep showing me that lady named Zophie in all my dreams?" Sia says, clearing her point.

Raul was confused by the last question and decided to ponder it to himself.

Suddenly, the bus stops and the driver starts speaking on the intercom.

"Attention all passengers, we have arrived at our destination. Our current location is Freemark and Saint Pete and the Saint Pete Mental Institution is the attraction of the area. Have a wonderful day," the bus driver says as he slowly rises from his seat and starts leading people out the door.

Sia and Raul both leave the bus together with their bookbags. Sia looks up at the institute in astonishment.

"Oh my Zeus, look at this place! It's kinda huge for a mental institution," Sia says mesmerized.

Raul looks at the institute in sadness. "My grandma is in here... she is who I came to see," Raul says as his voice begins to crackle.

Sia looks at Raul as if she wanted to cry. "Aww Raul, I don't even know what to say. How did your grandma get into this place?" Sia asks sympathetically.

Raul looks frustrated, but tries his best to control himself.

"She's... dangerous. I really don't want to get into detail, but she was a danger to me and my parents so my mom decided to lock her in here," Raul says, trying not to break down in tears.

Sia starts to feel awful for asking him about his grandma and decides to give Raul a hug.

"I am here for you. Let's go inside and see who we came here to see," Sia says confidently, trying to comfort Raul.

Raul looks at Sia and nods in agreement. Both Raul and Sia walk inside the mental institution to the front desk receptionist. The receptionist, Molly, cheerfully greets both Sia and Raul.

"Hello there! How can I assist you two today?" Molly says cheerfully.

Raul took the initiative to respond first. "I am here to visit Mrs. Bianca Kelp. She is my grandma," Raul says, showing his ID to Molly.

Molly takes his ID and searches up Mrs. Bianca Kelp on her computer. At last, Molly found the information she was looking for.

"Ahh yes Bianca Kelp. She is in room number 145 which is a right and then a left on the next corner," Molly says, directing Raul to his destination.

Raul goes immediately to his grandma's room without saying a word. Molly then turns her attention to Sia.

"And who are you here to see?" Molly asks as she waits for the name.

Sia starts to get butterflies in her stomach, but she does her best to remain calm.

"I am here to see Silver, I haven't seen her in so long and I miss her," Sia says, playing an innocent act to get what she wants.

Molly then searches up Silver and found multiple results.

"It appears we have three people in here with that name Silver Polanco, Silver Anderson, and a Silver Benington," Molly says, trying to find some answers.

Sia looks shocked hearing one of the Silvers having the same last name as hers, but she maintains composure.

"Silver Anderson is her name, Miss." Sia says, showing Molly her ID as well.

Molly then searches her computer for Silver Anderson to find some unsatisfying news.

"Oh dear, please give me a moment and I will be right back," Molly says with a slight look of concern.

Sia waits a few seconds and decides to wander off to find Raul. Sia walks by a room which can be seen from the outside through a glass window. A bookshelf and a bed is in the room with an old woman sitting on the bed. The old woman looks at peace from her face and her posture. The old woman looks at Sia through the window.

"Hello dear, what brings you to this place?" the old woman says pleasantly.

Sia looks at the old woman and gets closer to the window to respond.

"I'm just looking for a friend, he should be around here somewhere," Sia says, pondering.

The old woman chuckles. "Yes child, but you are also looking for something else," the old woman says again pleasantly.

Sia looks baffled. "What do you mean?" Sia asks curiously.

The old woman turns to Sia slowly. "You're looking for... the one that torments you?" the old woman says in a soft voice.

Sia looks even more confused. "Huh? How did you...?" Sia says, puzzled.

Just then, a dark entity possessed the old woman transforming the old lady into a red eyed, long pointy nailed version of herself. The demonic old woman rushes to the window with the speed of light and bangs the window loudly.

"ANSWER ME BITCH!" the demonic old woman says, continuously banging on the window and staring at Sia in the eyes.

Sia turns pale and jumps back in astonishment after witnessing such a horrendous transformation.

"OH MY ZEUS! WHO IS THIS WOMAN?" Sia says as she moves away from the window, staring at the woman.

Just then, Raul appears from the shadows of the hallway that Sia is currently in.

"This woman... is my grandma," Raul says as he approaches Sia, looking at his grandma through the window.

Sia jumps again in astonishment and looks at Raul.

"But... why is she... how did she...?" Sia says, baffled by the entire situation.

Raul looks at Sia seriously. "My parents told me that Grandma has been sick since I was a baby and it causes her to have these random freak outs, as they say. They told me there was no cure for her sickness so the best thing for them to do is to lock her in here forever. My parents lied to me; my grandma isn't sick at all. I learned that my grandma is possessed by a demon who controls her spirit at will," Raul says as he slowly stares back at his grandma.

Sia is still confused by his information. "That's horrible. How does one get possessed by a demon anyway?" Sia asks curiously.

Raul continues to stare at his grandma. "Demons are all around us. Sometimes people make deals with them to get what they want at a price, your soul. Sometimes you can be mentally vulnerable enough to allow them to possess you. The process is slower but it all starts with depression, stress and, frustration and eventually leads to homicidal and suicidal thoughts. However, in my grandma's case, I have no idea how she got this may and I may never know," Raul says, shedding tears while sharing what he knows.

Sia softly rubs Raul's back and smiles at him. "You're a great grandson for trying to figure out what your grandma is going through instead of just taking your parents' word for it. I'm proud of you," Sia says, looking up into his eyes and wiping his face with her thumb.

Raul smiles back at Sia and nods in approval. "Thank you Sia. You know for a tiny little pixie, you're alright in my book," Raul says, squeezing Sia's hand gently.

Sia blushes and punches Raul on his shoulder. "Hey! That's Captain Pixie to you mister. Have some respect," Sia says, joking sarcastically.

Raul laughs and took a seat next to his grandma's room in a daze. Sia decides to head back to the reception desk. Sitting at the reception desk was Molly who spotted Sia as she enters the room.

"There you are! I have been looking all over for you. I have to take you up to Silver Anderson's room, are you ready?" Molly says, concerned about Sia's well-being.

Sia smiles at Molly, feeling nervous about the situation. "Hehehe, sorry about that. I really had to go to the bathroom. Yes, I am ready to go. It's been so long," Sia says, still playing the part of her lie.

Molly approves and both Sia and Molly took an elevator up to the twenty-fourth floor. As the elevator opens, Sia sees the entrance of the door which looks like a laboratory for sick patients. Molly and Sia walk through a long hallway where you can see doors with locks the size of car tires and whispers on the other side of the doors. Sia tries to remain calm as they approach a door that says "Silver A. 666 HIGHLY CLASSIFIED" in the middle of it. Molly turns to Sia, showing her the door.

"Here we are. Reunions are such a beautiful thing," Molly says as she starts to unlock the door.

Sia waits nervously as Molly unlocks it. Molly unlocks the door, opens it, and puts her head inside and then quickly back out as if she saw something horrible.

"Oh my god, you cannot go in there," Molly says, looking at Sia in deep concern.

Just then, there was voice in the background that sounded like he was in distress. Molly looked over to notice a young boy running around that floor. Sia looked as well to notice it was Raul.

Molly looked agitated. "Hey you! You're not supposed to be up here!" Molly says, chasing the boy down the long hall way until they were no longer visible.

Sia realizes the door to Silver's room was still open and decides to go inside. Sia looks around the room to notice it was a purely white room with no windows. At the edge of the room, Sia saw a girl, Silver, sitting down staring at the ground wearing an all-white suit with a straightjacket. Sia slowly started to approach Silver until Silver suddenly made a sound.

"I've been... waiting for you... Sia," Silver says in a low tone.

Sia looked completely shocked and stopped in her tracks. "How do you... know my name?" Sia says, demanding some answers.

Silver slowly looks up at Sia and smirks. "Silly, you think I wouldn't recognize my own sister after this long?" Silver says, staring at Sia.

Sia looks baffled by her response. "Sister?! But... how? There's... no way," Sia says, extremely confused.

Silver shakes her head in disappointment and sighs. "I knew it... Zophie's parents got you brainwashed. They didn't tell you," Silver says, looking down at the ground again.

Sia moves a little closer to Silver as if she suddenly felt a connection.

"What haven't they told me? Who is Zophie and why have you been haunting my dreams?" Sia said, sternly demanding answers.

Silver looks at Sia slowly and signals Sia to sit next to her. Sia slowly approached Silver with tremendous fear and sat right beside her. Silver suddenly stares into space.

"You want the truth? I will help you as I promised you in your dream. There was... six of us. You and I came from the same father, our four little siblings came from a different father. We also had a stepbrother, but I never counted him as family.

He was Zophie's lap dog, getting *every* ounce of information she needed from him as a bribe to make sure she knew my every move and like a fool... I trusted him. Zophie was our mother, she's good at giving birth, but not so good at mothering," Silver says, notifying Sia of her past.

Sia starts to get curious. "What ever happened to them? I don't remember seeing these people in my life," Sia says, confused.

Silver looks at Sia slowly. "They met a gruesome fate, but you've seen what happened to them already," Silver says, reassuring Sia of Sia's nightmares.

Sia looks at Silver in complete shock. "So wait a minute, you mean to tell me... my nightmares..." Sia says, stuttering.

Silver cuts Sia off mid-sentence. "...Weren't actually nightmares. They were visions I gave to you so you know the truth about what happened when you were little. Did my actions frighten you, baby sis?" Silver says, slowly smirking at Sia.

Sia becomes skeptical. "No way that was real... my grandparents told me that my parents were coming to save me after their mission. I know they will!" Sia says confidently.

Silver sighs deeply. "And lemme guess, you have no idea what this mission is your parents are on?" Silver asks, folding her arms.

Sia looks at Silver as if she was a psychic with an accurate reading. "They... told me it was top secret," Sia says awkwardly.

Silver sighs again and looks at Sia. "Yeah, just like I was top secret too, huh? They never told you about me because I hold the truth and the truth is we don't have a family because I killed their sorry asses!" Silver says maniacally.

Sia stands up and looks at Silver seriously.

"WHY?! WHY DID YOU MASSACRE OUR ENTIRE FAMILY?!" Sia says, yelling at Silver sternly.

Silver continues to smirk at Sia. "Oh baby sis, our parents painted a perfect picture of our family, not knowing the torment they put us through. You were too young to understand so I got rid of them before it got any worse and spread to you," Silver says, reassuring Sia that she is on her side.

Sia, still confused, starts to grow more and more frustrated. "You poisoned our little siblings... they had nothing to do with the torment that our parents caused you!" Sia says as a rebuttal.

Silver shakes her head. "Those little brats were tools to use against us as we got older. Zophie considered you and I mistakes and those kids were her tools to belittle us and make us feel like unwanted garbage. They had to go!" Silver said sternly.

Sia sighs in frustration. "But... what about the other victims you killed in their sleep? What did they ever do to deserve that?" Sia says, raising her voice.

Silver continues to smirk. "Those fools? They tried to bully me when I was younger... they had it coming... I only left one alive so he can spread my aura around and it seems to have worked. And besides, didn't I look better with Carol's face on than she did?" Silver says nonchalantly.

Sia starts to turn red in frustration. "How bad could they have been for you to murder everybody in our family except our grandparents?" Sia says, yelling again.

Silver puts a serious face on and looks down. Silver suddenly pulls a sharp weapon from behind her, rips open her straight jacket, and dashes to Sia with insane speed holding the sharp object to Sia's neck.

"Respect your big sis, got it?" Silver says in a demented toned voice.

Sia is paralyzed and looks at Silver with fear with her hands up. "Y... Yes... sis," Sia says, quivering in fear.

Silver flips her sharp object back into her back pocket and sits back down smirking. "You should know me better than that, baby sis. That jacket was for show. No one can really trap me in here," Silver says, chuckling demonically.

Sia laughs back awkwardly, still feeling fear on the inside. Silver looks at Sia seriously.

"And about our grandparents... they are not what you think they are, baby sis," Silver says awkwardly.

Sia gives Silver a look of confusion. "Yes, I do know them. They love me very much!" Sia says with confidence.

Silver gives Sia a look of concern. "Don't be foolish, they caused a lot more harm than good. Ask yourself... why and how did you lose your memory? Why is it that you can't remember your own family?" Silver asks Sia in a serious tone.

Sia ponders on that question for a little while without any words to rebuttal. Silver moves closer to Sia.

"I can tell you why. John makes a serum that he injects in the back of the head of people to make them forget," Silver says as she rubs the back of Sia's head.

Sia looks baffled as she rubs the back of her head. "That... cannot be true. Would Grandpa really do that to me?" Sia asks in a daze.

Silver looks down. "Afraid so... he plays the fun grandpa, but deep inside he is a demanding, deceiving terror. I didn't bring you all this way to lie to you either," Silver says, enforcing the truth.

Sia ponders for a bit and then looks at Silver.

"Silver... why stay here when you can easily just escape?" Sia asks, confused.

Silver looks up at the ceiling. "I... deserve to be in here... all my actions, whether good or bad intentions, shall never go unpunished. Plus, as you already know... I'm a double S class arsonist with a power to manipulate dreams that no one understands. In reality... I'm just a freak of nature," Silver says, letting out a big sigh.

Sia looks at Silver sympathetically, without any words to say.

Silver looks at Sia and smiles. "We are connected in much more ways than you think. I think... you became someone who is very smart with a unique sense of style, I love... who you are... do you... like who you've become?" Silver says stuttering, holding Sia's hand with both of her hands.

Sia ponders a little on the question. "Well... sure I do. I feel as though I can be better but so far, I do love myself," Sia says, calming down a bit, but feeling a strange force coming out of Silver's hands.

Silver starts to cringe. "Do you realize... if Zophie was still alive... you wouldn't be this person at all. She would have made you into a bratty, stubborn little princess... her puppet... like she tried to make me, like she tried to make her four little spoiled rotten kids," Silver says, scratching the floor with her nails to relieve some anxiety.

Sia looks at Silver sympathetically, not knowing the whole story.

"Was Mom... Zophie... really as bad of a person as you made her out to be in my dreams?" Sia says softly, hoping for answers.

Silver looks at Sia with tears coming down her face.

"She tortured me my whole life, scaring me as I slept, kicking me out the house at only four years old until John... Grandpa... found me wandering outside alone. I wanted to be an artist and share my pictures with the world... Zophie destroyed my art along with my dream. I hate her so much, I decided to kill her twice in your dreams! She hated us both because we look like our father... After she was done with me... she was going to move on to you... and I was not going to accept my baby sister going through what I went through. I WON'T I WON'T," Silver says loudly as she started to bang the walls.

Sia started to shiver in fear watching her sister suddenly freak out. "Silver... sis... please calm down... who put you in this horrible place?" Sia says, trying to calm her down.

Silver stops banging the wall and turns to face Sia.

"The...only two people I left alive," Silver says as she falls to floor and passes out.

Sia runs to Silver and tries to see if she was okay.

Just then, Molly walks into the room to see Sia and Silver.

"What are you doing in here? It's far too dangerous to be in here! Lucky for you, you walked in here while she was sleeping," Molly says, escorting Sia out of Silver's room.

Sia was deep in thought while responding. "Yeah... lucky me." Sia says in a daze.

Molly continued closing the door to Silver's room and locking it shut, back to the way it was.

"Well, sorry you were disappointed that she was sleeping but... at least you got to see her," Molly says, trying make Sia feel better, not knowing the actual truth.

Sia smiles at Molly. "Yeah, you're right. I'm very happy I got to see her," Sia says with dark intentions in mind.

Molly smiles back and escorted Sia back downstairs to the main floor. Molly takes Sia to the main entrance lobby and says her goodbyes. Sia steps outside the mental institution and finds Raul sitting at the bus stop going back to Sia's home.

Sia approaches the bus stop and pokes Raul in the ear quietly, "Is this seat taken sir?" Sia says jokingly.

Raul looks at Sia and laughs. "It actually is. Don't sit on her. She gets offended," Raul says sarcastically, pointing at an empty seat.

Sia gives Raul and blank stare and then laughs it off, finally taking the empty seat. Sia looks at Raul seriously.

"Was that you who... made noises on that floor?" Sia asks awkwardly.

Raul smiles at Sia. "Dang, I guess I was too obvious, I tried to make myself sound like a sick monster or something," Raul says, feeling like a fool.

Sia laughs lightly. "Well... you definitely sounded sick that's for sure," Sia says, laughing a little more.

Raul laughs along and smiles. "The lady... said she wasn't going to let you in to see the girl you wanted to see so... I thought I would distract her so you could see her. I hope you were able to," Raul says, hoping his plan worked.

Sia gave Raul a big hug and a kiss on the cheek. "Yes, I was able to see her and talk to her in one piece. I know the whole truth now and it's all thanks to your brave, sick monster self," Sia says gratefully.

Raul blushes and smiles at Sia. "I'm really glad. Did you tell her off so she wouldn't give you anymore nightmares?" Raul asks, folding his arms.

Sia looks down. "Actually, it's so much more than that. It turns out... she is actually my sister," Sia says awkwardly.

Raul looks shocked at the news. "No way... what is she even doing there and... how did you not know you two were sisters?" Raul asks, intrigued.

Sia decides to explain the whole story to Raul, using the information Silver hadgiven to Sia.

Raul looks awfully concerned. "Wow, that is kind of screwed up... and I thought I had the dysfunctional family... sheesh," Raul says, rubbing Sia's back softly.

Sia awkwardly looks down. "I'm just upset that my grandparents couldn't tell me about any of this. Why would they hide this from me and pretend everything is alright?" Sia says, getting a bit frustrated.

Raul does his best to comfort her, not having any answers to give her. Just then, the bus arrives to pick up Sia and Raul as well as the other customers waiting for the bus. Sia and Raul go inside the bus and sit in the very back of the bus.

Raul looks at Sia seriously. "You know... you're going to have to confront your grandparents about this sometime," Raul says, trying to be realistic.

Sia pondered about that, knowing that with the information she knows now, she cannot hide it from her grandparents.

"You're right. What makes me scared is I feel like I don't know how I'm going to react when I see them after all this," Sia says, concerned about her own future actions.

Raul does his best to comfort Sia some more. "Just tell them how you feel, there is never anything wrong with that," Raul says, giving helpful advice.

Sia nods in agreement and decides to nod off and take a nap. However, she did not expect to find herself in yet another nightmare.

Sia wakes up in a two-floor house in a closed, empty closet. Sia starts to hear noises coming from downstairs that sound like thumping. Sia exits the closet and slowly makes her way downstairs. Just then, Sia starts to hear voices yelling at each other. Sia went to go peak from the corner of the other room to see both of her grandparents and Silver conversing.

"How could you do this?! My daughter? My grandbabies? Have you lost your goddamn marbles?!" Grandma Eva says, extremely angry.

Silver looks down and smirks. "Don't play dumb with me Eva, you know exactly why I did this. You think I would allow this torture to continue just like that? Endlessly, as you sit there and pretend that it didn't happen, not to my baby sister," Silver says confidently as she approaches both grandparents.

Eva gets frustrated. "Don't you dare bring her into this! You have no right defending someone you clearly don't care about!" Eva says, angrily shouting at Silver.

Silver starts to get defensive. "Are you naive? You think I would actually kill my baby sister? You are a bigger fool than I thought, old lady! She's been the only thing keeping me afloat and you think I would ever harm her?" Silver, says proving her love to her baby sister.

Eva wasn't buying it and folded her arms. Suddenly, Grandpa John got up from his seat and approached Silver.

"Well, you can't be around for us to find out, will we?" John says as he grabs Silver.

Silver started to get aggressive and attacked with a headbutt to John, leaving him with a bruise on his forehead. Silver then started to tussle with John, but was overpowered and pinned to the wall.

"John! You old, miserable bag of bones! What do you think you're doing!?" Silver says, fighting her way out of the arm bar.

John tightens up his hold. "Quick, get me a rope Eva!" John says, signaling to Eva.

Eva runs, opens a cabinet, and takes out a thick ball of rope. Sia panics, witnessing the big fight between John and Silver and runs back to Zophie's room, hiding in the closet once more. She runs back to find John on his feet and Silver passed out on the floor.

Eva panics. "Oh lord John! Did you seriously kill her?!" Eva says, checking Silver's pulse.

John chuckles. "Of course not, she's my grandbaby, so of course I would know her weaknesses. She's just asleep. Hand me the rope," John says, feeling a bit exhausted from his tussle with Silver.

Eva hands John the rope as John started to tie both her arms and legs up into a bind he knew she couldn't come out of. John lifted Silver over his shoulder.

"We need to lock her up in a place where no one would find her again," John says, pondering.

Eva agrees but also ponders. "We can't call the police because she got rid of all the evidence to make it look like a freak accident," Eva says, trying to figure out a solution.

John then finds a solution. "Alright, we will claim her as her legal guardian and put her in a mental institution where hopefully they don't release her for good behavior," John says, content with the plan.

Eva agrees to the plan. "Okay, we will do that. Should I... bother looking for Sia.. alive?" Eva asks, hoping Sia was still alive.

John agrees. "Yeah, she should be upstairs in Zophie's room where Zophie last texted us. Take this serum in case you see Sia alive. As soon as you see her, you inject it in the spot. I am going to put Silver in the back of the trunk," John says, pointing upstairs and slowly walks out the front door.

Eva slowly goes upstairs, trying not to step in any blood puddles. Eva enters Zophie's bedroom and saw what became of Zophie by the mirror.

"Oh lord... what a monster... evil spawn," Eva says, disgusted by the gruesome murder.

Eva starts to investigate the room until she heard a soft thump in the closet. Eva starts to approach the closet slowly.

"Sia? Sia? Is that you?" Eva says as she puts her hand on the closet door.

"Sia? Wake up Sia," Raul says, trying to awaken Sia from her sleep.

Sia then wakes up from her sleep and sees Raul. "What... what happened?" Sia says, trying to fully awaken.

Raul hands Sia's phone to her. "Someone is on the phone for you. You were too dead asleep to hear it," Raul says.

Sia takes the phone quickly and tries put her normal voice on.

"Hello? This is Sia," Sia says, answering her phone.

Sia's friend, Phoebe, was on the phone call.

"Sia! It's Phoebe! I got your message but I also have some bad news. Your grandma called my cell phone but my mother picked it up because I was in the shower and she told your grandma that you weren't here. Your grandma is on the way now to come look for you... I'm sorry, I tried to keep it a secret," Phoebe says, trying to plead her case.

Sia becomes pale and nervous about the outcome of her lie and what her grandma's reaction will be.

"Are you serious? Oh man... what am I going to say to her now?" Sia says, thinking of an excuse to tell her grandma.

Phoebe tries to ease Sia's conscience. "Don't worry Si Si, I will do my best to stall and find an excuse to make you seem innocent. Do you need directions to my house?" Phoebe says, trying her best to help.

Sia sighs heavily. "That's okay, just tell her that I went home if she shows up," Sia says in grief.

Phoebe agrees. "You got it girl, catch ya later!" Phoebe says as she hangs up the phone.

Sia puts her phone away and puts her head down in stress. Raul looks at Sia in concern.

"Hey... you okay?" Raul asks, trying to bring moral support.

Sia sighs and looks at Raul. "I guess so... something tells me I'm going to lose the last bit of family I have left," Sia says sadly.

Raul starts to comfort Sia. "Don't worry, everything will be alright as long as you find happiness within yourself," Raul says, trying to ease Sia's mood.

Sia looks at Raul in confusion.

"How can I find happiness when I have no family? Where is the happiness without family?" Sia asks as a rebuttal.

Raul looks Sia in her eyes and smiles. "You don't need anyone to be happy, Sia. There's a love in your heart for yourself that you don't even know about. You can unlock that by doing the things you love to do, whether there's people around you or not," Raul says, trying to help Sia.

Sia looks back at Raul and starts to move closer to him. "What makes you happy, Raul?" Sia says, softly looking deep into Raul's eyes.

Raul smiles at Sia and softly rubs her shoulder. "Art makes me happy. If I can create something out of nothing my whole life, I wouldn't need anything else. I'm sure there's something in this world you feel the same way about."

Sia ponders that for a while. "Perhaps, I always visioned myself falling for someone and getting married but... I never thought about what I would do if that never did happen," Sia says, deep in thought.

Raul smirks and chuckles a bit. "You always got to have a backup plan, not everything works out the way you think it would," Raul says, giving helpful advice.

Just then, a hard screech of car tires was heard nearby.

Suddenly, the driver of the bus shouts on his intercom, "EVERYBODY GET DOWN!"

The entire bus filled with people goes into panic as they scream and duck under their seats, including Sia and Raul. A truck crashes the bus at full speed, leaving the bus tumbling sideways until it stops on its side. The bus was completely destroyed, leaving few to no survivors. Sia wakes up in the destroyed bus bruised, but well enough to maneuver around. Sia looks around to see dead bodies squashed and smothered in titanium.

"Oy... what a... freak accident... Raul?" Sia says faintly, looking around for Raul.

Sia slowly continues to search around and sees Raul laying down, unconscious.

"Raul! Raul! Wake up! Let's get out of here," Sia says, attempting to wake up Raul.

Raul remained unconscious. Sia grabbed Raul's hand tightly and checked for a pulse. His hand was cold and he had no pulse. Sia begins to try harder to wake Raul up.

"Raul! This isn't funny! Wake up so we can get out of here... please," Sia says, trying to prevent thinking the worst.

Sia felt Raul's face and it was brick cold. Sia started to scream out of concern.

"Raul! Please don't leave me! Please wake up! Pleaseee! Raul!" Sia says, screaming at the top of her lunges, banging on Raul's chest, hoping to bring him back to life.

Sia starts to cry hysterically as she lays on Raul's chest. Sia gives Raul a long kiss on his lips as her tear drops fall on Raul's face.

"I will never forget you... I love you... Raul..." Sia says as she lets go of Raul's hand.

Sia slowly crawls out of the destroyed bus, bypassing all of the dead bodies along the way. Once Sia was out the bus, she got to her feet slowly and looked around to see police cars and ambulances approaching the scene in haste. Sia raises her arms so the ambulances can see her.

One of the ambulances stopped close to Sia and two nurses, Joe and Sara, came out of the ambulance, running towards Sia in extreme urgency.

"Are you alright? Can you walk?" Sara asks while trying to be delicate when touching Sia.

Sia folded both arms and started to cry. Joe came around with a stretcher for Sia. Sara rubs Sia's back gently.

"Come on sweetheart, let's get you to the hospital so you can feel better," Sara says, trying to comfort Sia.

Sia aggressively slaps Sara's hand off of her back. "Nothing will ever be okay! He's dead... the only one who really cared about me... the only one... who understands," Sia says heartbroken as she continues to cry.

Sara has a deep look of concern. "I know this has been really hard for you to deal with. You can talk to us about it on the way to the hospital, okay?" Sara says, again trying to calm Sia down.

Sia nods and walks to the ambulance with Sara and Joe. Once at the ambulance, Sia sits on the bed behind the ambulance with Sara.

Joe smiles lightly. "Well... I guess we really didn't need this for such a strong girl," Joe says as he puts the stretcher back in the ambulance.

Sia looks down speechless and stressed out. Joe then goes to the driver seat and starts to drive the ambulance. Sara tries to comfort Sia.

"Hey... I'm Sara. The bonehead driving the ambulance, his name is Joe. What's your name?" Sara says, trying to break the ice.

Sia slowly looks up at Sara.

"...Sia," Sia says uninterested.

Sara smiles at Sia. "Nice to meet you, Sia. You're a very brave and lucky girl to be able to survive such a horrible crash. Can you tell me the last thing you remember?" Sara asks, making conversation.

Sia looks back down. "I was talking to... my friend and... all of a sudden... a truck crashed into the bus we were in," Sia says, stuttering a bit.

Sara looks at Sia with a look of concern. "I see... and what happened to your friend?" Sara asks.

Sia suddenly becomes defensive. "DON'T ASK ME ABOUT MY FRIEND! HE DIDN'T DESERVE TO DIE! "Sia says assertively.

Sara backs off with her hands up. "Okay okay... no problem. Rest up, okay? We should be at the hospital soon," Sara says, trying to ease Sia.

Sia spaces out the entire trip to the hospital until they finally arrive. Sara opens the back door for Sia.

"We're here. Let's go get you checked out, okay?" Sara says calmly.

Sia walks out the ambulance without saying a word and starts following Sara inside of the hospital. As they walk inside, Sara looks at Sia.

"Is there any relative of yours we can call to pick you up?" Sara asks.

Sia nods. "Yeah... my grandparents." Sia says softly.

Sara approves. "Alright sounds good, may I have their numbers please?" Sara asks politely.

Sia nods, takes Sara's cellphone, and started typing her grandpa's cellphone number. Sia hands back Sara's cell phone.

"There ya go. That's my grandpa's number," Sia says.

Sara smiles at Sia. "Okay, I'll give them a call right now. Take a seat and rest, okay?" Sara says as she hands Sia a bag of ice for her bruises.

Sia nods and presses the ice on her bruises. Sitting next to Sia, there is an old woman looking at Sia.

"Are you okay, little one? Those bruises look awful," the old woman says, interested.

Sia looks at the old woman, confused.

"Yeah... I am fine, thanks. It's just a bruise," Sia says, trying to ease out of the conversation.

The old woman chuckles. "Yes, luckily it's only a bruise. You could've suffered the same fate as your friend," the old woman says.

Sia's eyes opened wide as she glares at the old woman.

"How did you.. know about that?" Sia says, demanding an answer. The old woman chuckles again. "Oh young lass, the question is not how I know this, the question is... how are you the only one who survived the bus accident?" the old woman says.

Sia ponders this and suddenly becomes speechless. The old woman suddenly has a sinister look on her face.

"She is watching you... she protects you and it is only because of her that you are still alive," the old woman says as she turns away and starts knitting her sweater.

Sia looked at the old woman in both confusion and shock. "What do you mean? Who's protecting me?" Sia asks, demanding more answers.

The old woman suddenly spaces out and doesn't answer Sia. Sia continues to look at the old woman, intrigued by her knowledge but also frustrated that she wouldn't answer her.

Suddenly, Sara walks back into the waiting room where Sia is.

"Hey Sia, your grandpa is here to pick you up," Sara says as she checks on Sia's bruises.

Just then, Sia's grandpa walks in and smiles at Sia.

"Hey pumpkin, how are you feeling?" John says, trying to comfort Sia.

Sia looks at her John with a dead stare.

"I'm okay. I just wanna go home," Sia replies.

John nods and helps Sia up and out of the hospital.

"Alright come on, let's take you home," John says.

Both Sia and Grandpa John enter his car and drive back to the house. During the trip, John tries to make small talk with

Sia, but Sia was spaced out and didn't respond to anything the whole trip. After a thirty minute drive, John and Sia finally make it home. As they walk inside, Grandma Eva greets them at the door.

"Welcome home honey!" Eva says, excited.

Sia stares dead into space without any reaction.

Eva looks at Sia concerned. "Are you okay sweetheart? These bruises look awful. Did your friend do this to you?" Eva says, trying to ease Sia's bruises.

Sia looks at John slowly. "You haven't told her... have you?" Sia asks with a serious look on her face.

Eva looks at both Sia and John. "What do you mean? What happened?" Eva asks, demanding answers.

John was going to answer, but just then Sia cut John off.

"I got into a bus crash and survived with these bruises. But he's not the only one keeping secrets... right John?" Sia says, staring at John.

John and Eva were both side-eyed as they both stared at Sia.

Eva approached Sia slowly. "Um dear... how did you know Grandpa's name?" Eva asks Sia, stuttering a little.

Sia looks at Eva with a serious look. "Oh... I know plenty about this family... the only thing I want to know is... why haven't you ever told me about my sister?" Sia asks nonchalantly.

John and Eva were speechless as they remained wide eyed from the information that Sia knew. Eva jumps around Sia's question.

"Who is telling you this information? How did you know about this?" Eva asks anxiously.

Sia starts to get frustrated. "Answer the fucking question Eva! You kept secrets from me and now I wanna know why?!" Sia asks, screaming angrily.

John steps in front of Eva and looks at Sia. "Okay, you want to know the truth? Fine. your so called sister killed our entire family for whatever her personal reasons are, so we had no choice but to lock her up in a place where she couldn't kill us or you either," John says bluntly, standing in front of Eva.

Sia's eye starts to twitch. "Did you even know why she killed them? Have you ever bothered to figure out what drove her to that point? Sitting down with her and asking her?" Sia asks, folding her arms.

Eva remained speechless as John continues to rebut.

"She was troubled and sick in the head, there was no other choice," John says, trying to calm Sia down.

Sia gets more frustrated. "Oh sure... that's the reason. She wasn't 'troubled' nor 'sick in the head' when she was a little girl. She was turned into the monster she is today by her very own family!" Sia says, stating her point.

John chuckles. "Is that right? And how did you come to THAT conclusion?" John asks in suspense.

Sia looks at John deep in his eyes. "You let your daughter destroy her emotionally and spiritually. You let Zophie try to manipulate Silver into becoming something she never wanted to be and because of it, Zophie decided to make Silver's life a living hell The saddest part about it all is... you both drugged me so I wouldn't know ANY of this... why?" Sia says, demanding an answer.

John takes a step back after hearing all the information Sia has brought to him and realizes Sia knows the whole truth. John walks back next to a cabinet.

"Well... it seems you know everything pumpkin. Are you proud of yourself? I'm sorry that it has to be this way," John says as he takes out a knife from the cabinet.

Eva stands back against the wall, trembling in fear. Sia is suddenly wide-eyed watching John slowly approach her with his knife.

"Grandpa... what are you doing with that thing?" Sia asks slowly, starting to quiver.

John has a demented look on his face. "What I should've done a long time ago," John says as he raises his knife to Sia.

Suddenly, a butcher knife flies through the window of the house, catching John right on the side of the head. John falls to the ground with blood spewing out of his head, getting a little on Sia's face and clothes. Sia has a look of both shock and confusion. Eva screams in utter horror as she watches her husband die before her eyes. Eva then stares at Sia.

"How... how could you do this to your own grandfather?" Eva says in complete torment.

Sia looks at Eva confused. "But... you just saw I didn't do anything." Sia pleads innocently.

Eva continues to tremble against the wall. "Don't play stupid with me. You're no different from that bitch you call a sister!" Eva says furiously.

Just then, a loud sniper rifle gunshot can be heard as it pierces through the window of the house and enters Eva's skull. Eva's body falls to the floor and blood spews from her brain. Sia falls to ground in complete shock, watching both of her grandparents dead on the floor, not knowing exactly what caused this to happen. Sirens are heard approaching Sia's house in haste as police cars and ambulance stop right in front. Police men approach the front door and kick it down, finding Sia on her knees covered in her grandparents' blood.

"Are you hurt?" One of the policemen asks Sia.

Sia was too traumatized to answer. The policemen take Sia out of the house and started to investigate the scene. The police tried asking Sia a series of questions but she will not answer. The police then decide to take Sia down to the station for further questioning. A few hours later, a group of detectives gather around a room.

"There was a surveillance tape at the Anderson house, I think you guys might wanna take a look at this," the detective says, playing the tape on the big screen.

The video showed Sia and John arguing for a few minutes. After a quick reaction from John, he goes to grab the knife from the kitchen cabinet. As John goes to turn around, Sia pulls out a butcher knife from the back of her shirt and swings it at John's head, leaving the butcher knife stuck on his head. You can then hear Eva screaming loudly in the background. Sia's eyes turn pitch black and she then took out what looks to be a sniper rifle from under the living room couch. Sia slowly aims at Eva and shoots her right on the temple. Sia then drops the gun and falls to her knees, heavy breathing deeply and slowly looks at the camera with a demented stare.

The video ends there as all the detectives look at each other as if they know what to do. Two detectives, Ross and Howard, leave the meeting room and walk to the room where Sia is being held. Both detectives walk inside the room and see Sia sitting there spaced out. Ross decides to sit down and look at Sia.

"Young lady, you do realize what you have done, right?" Ross says bluntly.

Sia shakes her head slowly while still staring into space.

Ross puts pictures of John and Eva's corpse after the murder scene on the table for Sia to see.

"You killed the only relatives you have and for what? That's what I want YOU to tell me," Ross says, waiting for an answer.

Sia slowly looks at Ross with a demented stare. "Do you… really wanna know?" Sia says, stuttering.

Ross sits back and folds his arms, staring at Sia. "Obviously, that's the reason I asked you in the first place," Ross says, a little agitated.

Just then, Sia smirks demonically as she takes out a sharp object from her back pocket and swiftly slices Ross's neck wide open. Ross deeply gasps for air as he holds on to his neck with eyes wide open, he falls to the ground slowly dying. Howard starts to panic as he tries to run out of the room.

When Howard reaches for the door knob, Sia jumps on Howard's back and stabs him in both eyes, leaving both eyeballs stuck to Sia's sharp object. As Howard screams and bleeds to death, Sia slowly starts to transform into Silver.

Once Sia fully transformed, Silver then licks the blood from her sharp object and brings out a demented smile. "I wanted them to bleed like me."